RACING STRIPES

Adapted by Tracey West
from the screenplay by David Schmidt

Scholastic Inc.

New York   Toronto   London   Auckland   Sydney
Mexico City   New Delhi   Hong Kong   Buenos Aires

ISBN 0-439-71874-0

Designed by Rick DeMonico

12   11   10   9   8   7   6   5   4   3   2   1   5   6   7   8   9/0

Printed in the U.S.A.
First printing, January 2005

It was a stormy night. The circus was leaving town.

But one of the circus trucks broke down. A baby zebra was left behind by mistake.

A man named
Nolan found the baby
zebra on the road.
Nolan took him home
to his farm.

Nolan put the zebra in the barn. The other animals came to see him.

"I have never seen anything like it," said Franny, a goat.

Tucker, a pony, shook his head.

"It is just a funny-looking horse,"he said.

Reggie the rooster laughed. "You two are pretty funny-looking, too," he said.

Nolan's daughter, Channing, came to see the zebra. She fed him from a bottle. Then she gave him a name.

"Welcome to your new home, Stripes," she said.

Stripes grew up on the farm. He did not know he was a zebra. He thought he was a horse.

One day, Stripes saw horses racing each other at the racetrack.

"They are getting ready for the Big Race," Tucker told him. "Every year, horses race to see who is the best."

7

Stripes never forgot about the big race. He wanted to race more than *anything*!

Every day, Stripes raced the mail truck. He usually won. But one day, he saw a beautiful pony walk by. Stripes forgot about the truck. He ran into a tree!

The pony smiled at Stripes. "Maybe you should go around that tree next time," she said. "I'm new here. My name is Sandy."

"I'm Stripes," Stripes said shyly. "I'm a racer! Well, I just race around here, mostly."

Two horses from another ranch heard Stripes.
"You are no racer," said Ruffshod.
"He only races himself," Pride teased.
"I'll race you any time you want!" Stripes said.
Then Sir Trenton, Pride's father, trotted up.
He scolded the two younger horses. "This beast
is beneath you. You have better things to do."

But Pride did not listen to his father. He challenged Stripes to a secret race that night.

When it was dark, Stripes showed up at the Blue Moon Races. Pride and Stripes raced around the valley.

Stripes was fast — really fast. He bolted ahead of Pride.

But then came a sharp turn. Stripes was going too fast. He slid in the mud and fell. Pride won!

The next day, Stripes was feeling sad. But a new visitor came to the farm — a pelican!

"My name is Goose," said the pelican. "I come from the big city. I'm the baddest bird around."

Goose tried to show everyone what a great flyer he was. Instead, he flew right into the barn!

While Goose flapped around, Stripes and Tucker talked.

"I want to race Pride again," said Stripes. "For real."

"You need a rider for that," said Tucker.

"I wish Channing didn't ride that iron horse of hers," Stripes said, looking at Channing's motorbike. "Then she would have to ride me."

"I can fix that," Goose said.

Goose broke Channing's motorbike. So Channing rode Stripes to the racetrack, where she worked.

But Clara, the owner of the racetrack, did not want Stripes there.

"That thing belongs at a zoo!" she sniffed.

Stripes felt sad.

Buzz and Scuzz, two horseflies, tried to cheer him up.

"I have never seen a black horse with white stripes before," said Scuzz.

"Don't be silly. He is a white horse with black stripes!" said Buzz.

Soon it was time to go home. But Channing had an idea.

She took Stripes for a ride around the empty racetrack.

They didn't know it, but someone was watching. . . .

Woodzie, a race fan, walked up to Channing and Stripes.

"That is one fast animal," Woodzie said. "You should bring him to the practice races in the morning."

Channing took Stripes to the practice race the next morning. Some news reporters noticed Stripes right away.

"Is that what I think it is?" one of them asked.

Stripes lined up for the race. But he was used to racing on the farm, not at the track. The big starting gate scared him. He did not know which way to go.

But Channing got Stripes under control. Soon he was speeding down the track!

Then Stripes got scared again. He did not know how to get past the horses in front of him.

Stripes reared up — and Channing fell off his back!

Channing's dad ran up to Channing. She was not hurt.

The news reporters grouped around Clara, the owner of the track.

"Will you let the zebra run in the big race?" a reporter asked her.

"Why not?" said Clara. "There is no way he can win."

"Did you hear that?" Sir Trenton asked Stripes. "The racetrack is no place for a zebra."

"What did you call me?" Stripes asked.

"A zebra," said Sir Trenton. "You didn't really think you were a horse, did you?"

But Stripes *did* think he was a horse. Sadly, he walked away.

Back home, Nolan agreed to let Channing and Stripes enter the big race. Channing worked hard to get Stripes ready.

But Stripes did not want to enter the big race anymore. Now he knew he was a zebra, not a racehorse.

"I can't do this!" Stripes moaned.

"That's enough," Franny said. "Tucker believes in you. He has trained all of the race-horses that Nolan used to own. He can train you, too."

"Tucker, do you really think I have what it takes?" Stripes asked.

"You don't have the body of a racehorse. But you have more heart than any of them," Tucker said. "I know you can do it!"

Tucker helped Stripes train. Soon came the day of the big race.

Sandy, Franny, and all of Stripes's friends from the farm went to the track to cheer him on.

Pride and Ruffshod teased
Stripes before the race started.

"Do you really think you can
race, freak?" Ruffshod asked.

But Stripes just ignored them.
He wanted to race — not fight.

B-r-r-ring! The race started. The horses ran through the gate.

Ruffshod tried to cheat. He ran close to Stripes so Stripes could not get ahead.

Scuzz flew out to help. The horsefly bit Ruffshod.

It worked! Ruffshod reared up. His rider fell off. Ruffshod was out of the race!

Stripes was way behind. But he didn't give up. He rode faster and faster . . .

"Look at that zebra go!" said the race announcer. "Now Stripes is neck-and-neck with Pride!"

Stripes and Pride ran across the finish line. The race was too close to call. It was a photo finish!

Everyone waited for the judge's decision. Then the results flashed on the scoreboard.

"Stripes, you did it!" Channing cheered. "You won!"

Stripes smiled. It felt good to win.
And he couldn't have done it without
all of his friends!